Mr. Monkey
Visits a School

Jeff Mack

Simon & Schuster Books for Young Readers
New York   London   Toronto   Sydney   New Delhi

For my mom, a great teacher, a great mom. Ooh! Ooh!

SIMON & SCHUSTER BOOKS FOR YOUNG READERS
An imprint of Simon & Schuster Children's Publishing Division
1230 Avenue of the Americas, New York, New York 10020
SIMON & SCHUSTER BOOKS FOR YOUNG READERS is a trademark of Simon & Schuster, Inc.
For information about special discounts for bulk purchases, please contact Simon & Schuster Special Sales at
1-866-506-1949 or business@simonandschuster.com.
The Simon & Schuster Speakers Bureau can bring authors to your live event.
For more information or to book an event, contact the Simon & Schuster Speakers Bureau
at 1-866-248-3049 or visit our website at www.simonspeakers.com.
Book design by Chloë Foglia and Jeff Mack
The text for this book was set in Century Schoolbook.
The illustrations for this book were rendered digitally.
Manufactured in China
0418 SCP
First Edition
2 4 6 8 10 9 7 5 3 1
Library of Congress Cataloging-in-Publication Data
Names: Mack, Jeff, author, illustrator.
Title: Mr. Monkey visits a school / Jeff Mack.
Other titles: Mister Monkey visits a school
Description: First edition. | New York : Simon & Schuster Books for Young Readers, [2018] | Series: Mr.
Monkey | Summary: Mr. Monkey is invited to visit a school to
perform a trick he just learned, but nothing goes as planned.
Identifiers: LCCN 2017023010| ISBN 9781534404298 (hardcover) | ISBN 9781534404304 (eBook)
Subjects: | CYAC: Monkeys—Fiction. | Tricks—Fiction. | Schools—Fiction. | Humorous stories.
Classification: LCC PZ7.H83727 Mrv 2018 | DDC [E]—dc23
LC record available at https://lccn.loc.gov/2017023010

Mr. Monkey learns a trick.

Almost.

He tries it again.

OOH.

And again.

OOH!

OOH!

He gets it!

Now he's ready to put on a show!

Mr. Monkey combs his hair.

He brushes his teeth.

He puts on a snazzy tie.

And he walks out to his car.

But he forgets one thing. . . .

Much better, Mr. Monkey.

Mr. Monkey drives to school.

He stops.

BEEP!
BEEP!

MOO.

Move, cow! Move!

Mr. Monkey lifts.

He tosses.

He moves the cow.

Mr. Monkey walks to school.

It starts to rain.

Mr. Monkey has an idea.

It starts to snow.

It starts to snow more.

The snow won't stop Mr. Monkey.

He slides to the school.

He slides faster.

And faster!

Mr. Monkey falls.

Mr. Monkey flaps.

Mr. Monkey flies to the school!

Mr. Monkey is ready for the show.

He goes inside.

He meets some new friends:
The crossing guard.

The gym teacher.

The principal.

And the librarian.

Uh-oh!
Where did Mr. Monkey's stuff go?

Mr. Monkey can't do his trick without his stuff.

Mr. Monkey takes the stage.

The kids are ready.

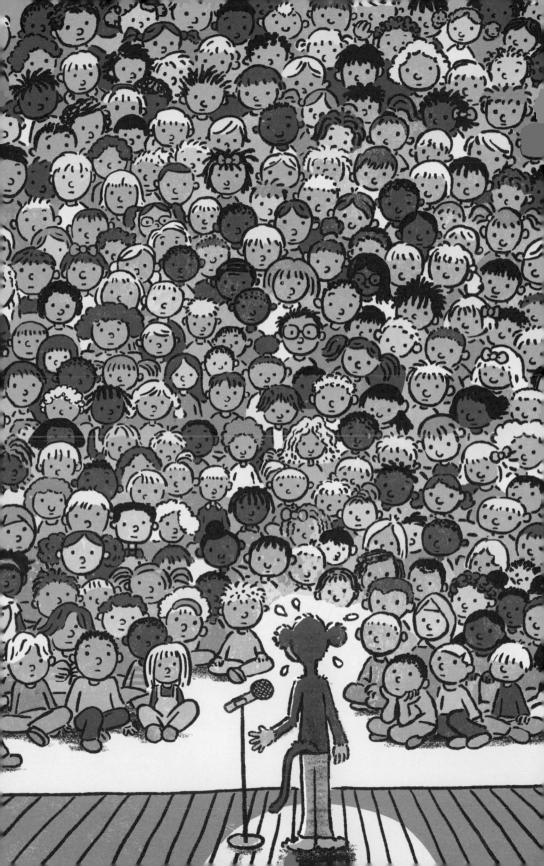

They all want to see his trick.

But what will he do?

Mr. Monkey runs away.

He comes back.

He catches the cow!

He tries it again.

And again!

He does it!
Mr. Monkey does a new trick!

Almost.

The librarian is not so sure
she likes this new trick.

But what about the kids?

They like it!